ROBINSON CRUSOE

DANIEL DEFOE

ADAPTED BY SAVIOUR PIROTTA · ILLUSTRATED BY ALESSANDRO BALDANZI

Disaster at Sea

I was born in 1632, in the English city of York. My father was very keen for me to become a lawyer, but I was far more interested in going to sea. As soon as I was old enough, I boarded a ship bound for distant lands.

For a while, my seafaring brought me luck and fortune. I bought goods in one port and sold them in another, making a huge profit. I even managed to buy a coffee plantation in Brazil. Then one day I was sailing along the coast of South America, when our ship was caught in a storm.

The wind blew us off course so when the captain saw land through his telescope he did not know where we were. Hoping to find shelter, he steered the ship towards the land. Alas, we hit sand in shallow water long before we reached the shore. In no time at all the ship was flooded and sinking. We hastily lowered a small boat into the heaving waves.

However, the sea was so rough that the boat was soon overturned. We were flung into the sea and I began swimming. I don't know how long I struggled in the sea, but I do remember it was starting to get dark when I felt sharp pebbles under my feet.

By some miracle, I had made it to shore alive. Coughing up water, I dragged myself out of the sea and crawled up on to gritty sand.

Alone and Lost

I searched the deserted beach but there was no sign of my companions from the ship. Then a horrible thought struck me: what if there were dangerous creatures that would pounce on me and tear me limb from limb? I had to find somewhere safe to spend the night. I hurried up the beach to a tropical jungle. There I climbed into a tree and, settling down on a huge branch, fell into a deep sleep.

When I woke up, the sun was shining. The wind had dropped and the sea was calm. To my amazement, I could see our wrecked ship. The wind and tide had brought it closer to shore and she was trapped on a sandbar.

I called out, hoping one of my companions would answer back. No one did. I was alone. Alone and lost! I had no idea if I was back on the coast of South America or stranded on a small island. No one had come to take a closer look at the wreck. That meant the place must be uninhabited. I didn't have a single soul to share my troubles with.

For a while I sat on a rock, feeling sorry for myself. Then I said to myself, "Cheer up. Do you not realize how lucky you are? Your shipmates are all dead but you are still alive. If you are to survive till a ship passes by, you are going to need all your skills."

Back on Board

My first task was to find fresh water. Nothing had passed my lips for hours and I was parched. I set off into the jungle, which was quite hilly and filled with flowers of every shape and colour. Once I had found a spring of fresh water, I had a long drink and washed my face and hands. Nearby the birds were feasting on strange fruit the size of my fist.

I plucked one and, squashing it open with my fingers, ate the ripe flesh. I didn't know what the fruit was called but it was delicious. Picking some more, I stuffed them into my pockets for later and returned to the shore.

By now the tide was low, and the wrecked ship looked so close I knew I could swim to it. I waded out as far as I could, then swam towards it.

The next time I looked up, the hull was towering above me. I could see a rope dangling over the side, its end knot just within reach. Grabbing it with both hands, I hauled myself up. A loud bark greeted

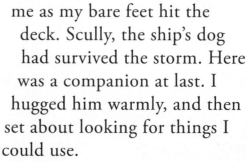

me as my bare feet hit the deck. Scully, the ship's dog had survived the storm. Here was a companion at last. I hugged him warmly, and then set about looking for things I could use.

In the food chest, I found bread and cheese, and dried goat's meat cut into strips. There was a bag of wheat too, which the cook had meant to grind into flour. I also found the cook's knife, stuck in a big cheese.

From the storeroom, I dragged out a carpenter's chest full of tools. I also took a couple of swords, some muskets, a bag of shot and a cask of gunpowder. They would all come in handy if I needed to go hunting.

In the captain's cabin I found a bag of silver coins and a Bible. I took the holy book and also the coins with me, even though I couldn't imagine what use money would be on an uninhabited island.

Once I had piled all the things on deck, I had to find a way to get them safely to shore. There were lots of wooden planks floating around the ship. I lashed them together with rope and made a raft.

Then I carefully lowered my goods on to it. When the tide came in, I climbed down, taking the dog with me, and hoped the current would carry me to land.

As I sat down on the carpenter's chest, I felt a thump behind me. The dog barked, and I turned to see the ship's cat had joined us.

My little family was growing.

My Island Home

After a quick lunch, I climbed to the top of the hill to get my bearings. My new home was a small island. There were no houses, no sign of habitation, just dense jungle. I could see land far away across the sea, but I could not tell whether it was the coast of South America or just a bigger island.

During the climb, I also found the perfect spot to pitch my camp. It was a flat piece of land, halfway up a hill overlooking the beach I had landed on. From there I could see out over the ocean, but anyone approaching the island would not see me unless I wanted them to. My little piece of land, my new home, was well screened with bushes. Clean water trickled in a stream nearby.

I hurried back down to the shore and, one by one, fetched the goods I had salvaged. I arranged them all around me in a circle, the dog sitting on the carpenter's chest, the cat licking her paws on the cask of gunpowder. It was dark now, and I was tired. I read the Bible for a while, thanking God for all the provisions he had sent me, and for rescuing me from the storm.

And then I slept.

During the next few days, I ventured out to the wrecked ship no less than twelve times. I managed to bring back some heavy canvas and bits of sail that had been ripped off by the storm.

I also found more tools and ammunition for my guns, wooden buckets, the cook's grindstone, some fishing hooks and line, and a battered telescope. Going back to my old quarters to retrieve my hammock, I found another cat lying in it. I scooped it up and carried it to the raft.

The poor creature was lucky I found her that day. The same night, a sudden storm blew up and smashed our ship to pieces.

The next day I used the canvas to make a proper tent, in which I strung out my hammock. But I still didn't feel secure against any wild beast that might come charging over the hills.

So I set about building a wooden wall, a palisade, around my tent. I did this by hacking trees into stakes and driving them into the ground. Soon I had my own little fortress to protect me. There was no door or gate. I made a wooden ladder, which I lifted after me every time I went in or out of my new home.

I also hollowed out a little cave in the hill behind me. I put all the gunpowder I had rescued from the ship in the cave, so it would not get damp in the rain.

I realized that I would soon lose track of time unless I kept a record. On the exact spot where I had crawled out of the water, I hammered a wooden post in the ground. This became my calendar. Every day, I carved a notch in it with my knife.

Time passes quickly when you have so many things to do. I built myself a chair and table. My old clothes were becoming ragged, so I sewed new ones from the bits of ragged sail. I caught wild hares to eat, and made clothes from fur. I even made myself a large umbrella to keep the hot sun off my face.

I grew wheat from the grain I had found in the cook's store and made flour from it. That first mouthful of bread, baked in a clay oven I made, tasted better than anything I had ever eaten.

One day I found a goat caught in one of my rabbit traps. It was bleating so sadly, I released her. She followed me home, with her kids trotting after her. From that day I never lacked for fresh milk and even learned to make cheese.

I trapped a parrot which I named Poll. He loved snatching food out of my hand, but, try as I might, I could not get him to say a word.

And so the notches on the wooden post increased, until five years had passed and my skin had turned a deep, nutty brown.

The Canoe

One day I had an idea to build a canoe. It might carry me across the sea to the distant land I could see from the top of the hill.

I felled a large cedar tree with my axe and started hollowing it out. It was back-breaking work. Chopping the tree down took a month, hollowing it out another three months. But at last I finished it. Now all I had to do was drag it down to the water. This is when I realized I'd made a big mistake.

The canoe was too far from the beach, and too heavy to drag across stony ground. I thought about digging a channel from the shore to it but I calculated it would take at least twelve years to finish. So I abandoned the canoe, and with it all hope of leaving the island. As I cooked my dinner that night, I felt lonelier than I ever had in my entire life. But as I sat down to my meal, a shrill voice made me jump.

"Poor Robinson Crusoe. Poor Robinson Crusoe. Where are you, Robinson Crusoe?"

It was Poll the parrot. He had spoken at last, but they were not words I had tried to teach him. Then I remembered that I talked to myself like that when I was feeling sad about being stuck on the island. Poll had copied me, and the sound of his voice was a greater comfort to me than anyone could imagine.

Visitors

A year or so after I had abandoned my canoe, I started building a much smaller sailing boat. It gave me great pleasure to sail around my little island, discovering new coves and beaches. But it would never take me across the sea.

One day I was walking to my boat when I saw a footprint in the sand. For a moment I thought it was my own. Then I realized that the foot that had made it was much smaller than mine.

There was someone else on the island, someone who had arrived unnoticed. I shivered in my furry clothes. Who could this stranger be? Where on the island was he hiding? And was he friendly, or a man-eating cannibal?

I hurried home to fetch my telescope. Then, making sure the dog or the goats were not following, I set out to explore every inch of the island. If I had a visitor, I wanted to know where he was.

That afternoon, I ventured much further from my little fortress than I had ever done before. In some parts of the island the hills were very steep and I'd had no reason to climb them before. That day, reaching the top of one, I put the telescope to my eye and looked out to sea. There was a boat bobbing on the waves, a canoe with perhaps six or eight people – I couldn't tell exactly how many this far away. They were paddling away from my island, their backs to me.

I watched until the boat disappeared into the distance. Now I could smell smoke wafting up from the beach below. I hurried down, towards the remains of a bonfire I could see in the sand. When I came close to it, I stopped and stared in horror. The ashes from the fire were still smouldering, and scattered all around were skulls and the remains of other human bones.

The sight of those charred bones chilled me to the core. I had heard about cannibals before. I knew they were dangerous, and I was determined not to be captured by them.

Returning home, I decided to start burning charcoal instead of wood on my cooking fire. It would make less smoke that could be seen by the cannibals. Looking for wood to make charcoal, I stumbled across the mouth of a tunnel, hidden behind some bushes at the foot of a hill.

I managed to wriggle inside, and discovered it led to the most amazing underground cave. The walls and roof were covered in stalactites, which glittered like multicoloured jewels in the light of a candle I had brought with me.

Here was a safe hiding place for my guns and powder. It would make perfect sleeping quarters too if the cannibals ever returned. Once inside the tunnel, I could easily block up the entrance with a rock.

A Daring Rescue

Luckily many years passed and the cannibals did not return. Scully the dog and the cats grew old and died. Poll the parrot passed away too, and I caught and tamed some more birds, which, together with my growing herd of goats, kept me company. If I had not been worried that the cannibals might return, I believe I would have been quite happy to stay in that little paradise for the rest of my life.

Then one day I saw a wisp of smoke rising above the trees some two miles up the coast. My heart skipped a beat. Was it the cannibals again?

I fetched my telescope and a musket, and keeping to the shadow of the trees, crept along the coast. I stopped above a creek where I had often come to fish. On the other side of it, I could see no less than thirty men dancing round a fire. They had two canoes pulled up on the sand. Tied to a tree nearby were two other men.

Three of the dancing men approached the tree and, whooping loudly, slashed the ropes holding the prisoners. One was immediately hit on the head with a club. The other, finding himself free for a moment, screamed and sprinted towards the creek.

Three of the cannibals around the fire grabbed their bows and arrows and ran after him. They came to the water and two dived into the creek after the fugitive, their bows slung over their shoulders.

Quickly, I slid from my hiding place and, after waiting for the escaped prisoner to clamber out of the water, rushed at the men chasing him. I hit the first one with the end of the telescope and sent him reeling back into the creek. The second one, though, saw me and leaped sideways on to the beach.

His hand reached out to the bow on his shoulder. I knew he meant to shoot me, so I whipped out my musket and fired at him.

The blast from my gun made the fugitive rigid with shock. His eyes grew wide and he stared in horror at my musket. I patted him on the shoulder and smiled to show that I was a friend.

"We'd better go if you don't want to be captured again," I said out loud.

And then I turned and ran back into the trees. The man followed me, mostly because the cannibals on the beach were starting to run towards us.

Before long we reached the safety of my hideout, and the man fell to his knees in front of me. He placed my foot on his head to show me that I was now his master.

"Now, now," I said, pulling him to his feet. "I need a friend, not a slave. My name is Robinson Crusoe. What is yours?"

The man did not seem to understand. "Today is Friday," I said. "Your lucky day. I think I shall call you Friday."

Friday

The next day Friday and I returned to the creek to see if the cannibals had left. There was no sign of them, or their canoes. The traces of their fire were still visible though, and the beach was littered with bones.

"Is it not horrific?" I said to Friday. But he did not seem at all upset at the sight of the human remains. I suspected he too had eaten human flesh in the past.

I was determined to educate my new friend, so I roasted a goat over the fire and gave him the meat to eat on some bread. His eyes shone at the taste of it.

"Goat, good," I said.

"Goat, good," he repeated.

I pinched the flesh on my arm.

"Man-flesh, not good."

"Man-flesh, not good," echoed Friday.

Still, I knew I'd be foolish to trust the fellow just yet. I made him a tent to sleep in outside the palisade.

So began one of the happiest times of my life. I set about teaching Friday to speak English. I taught him how to grow crops and tame birds. I also spoke to him about my belief in God.

Soon I realized I did not need to worry about Friday harming me. He was loyal and trustworthy, and the best friend I'd ever had. Once he'd learned enough English to hold a proper conversation, we often talked long into the night.

One day, I said to him, "Do you not wish to see your own country again?"

"Yes," he replied, "but I will only go if you come with me, sir."

After supper, I took him to see the enormous canoe I had made many years before. The wood had split over the years and most of it was rotten.

"Will a boat like this be able to take us across the sea to your country?" I asked.

"Yes," said Friday, and the next day we set about building another canoe, closer to the water this time. I let Friday choose the tree, for I realized he knew much more about seafaring than I did. When it had been chopped down, we hollowed it out, using the old axe I had rescued from the ship. I made a mast, and a sail out of the old canvas. Friday carved an oar, which would come in handy if the wind dropped while we were out at sea. After several months it was finally finished.

I had now been on the island for twenty-seven years. I was so used to it by now that the idea of leaving almost frightened me. Still, with the canoe finished, we started packing it with goods and tools we would take with us.

One morning I told Friday to go down to the beach and look for turtle eggs, to add to our provisions. He came back trembling.

"There are bad men on the beach again."

The Pale Prisoner

I handed him the axe and, fetching my muskets, swords and the telescope, we hurried to the very spot where I had seen Friday for the first time. This time there were twenty-one cannibals by the creek. They had arrived in two canoes, which had been secured with rope to a tree stump at the water's edge. A prisoner was kneeling on the sand, and he was pale, like me. A European! He had his hands tied behind his back and his legs bound together at the ankles.

"Follow me," I whispered to Friday, shutting the telescope.

We crept down to the beach, where the cannibals were building a fire. Hiding behind a bush, I handed Friday one of the muskets.

"I trust you'll be able to use one of these," I said. "You've seen me shooting hares often enough."

"I'll try my best," whispered Friday.

"Good. You aim at the men on the right, I'll aim at the ones on the left."

We both fired at the same time and five of the cannibals fell to the ground. The rest of them leaped to their feet and, unable to see what had killed their companions, started running about in panic.

30

"Now is our chance. Go for the prisoner," I hissed at Friday, and we both ran to the poor man. I took out my knife and slashed the ropes binding the pale man's hands. Then I freed his feet.

"Do you have enough strength to help us?" I asked in Portuguese.

He understood and nodded. I thrust a sword in his hands. Friday, meanwhile, had continued firing at the other cannibals, who were rushing towards their canoes.

"Let's follow the beasts and finish them off," he howled.

The three of us ran after the cannibals and, before they could push out their boats, we had cut down two more of them. The others fled in one of the canoes, wailing, their eyes wide with fear.

Friday was about to leap into the second canoe, when he stopped suddenly. He had found another prisoner in the boat. We hadn't seen him because he'd been lying down, his feet and legs tied together.

Friday helped him to his feet and cut the bindings. When he turned to me, Friday had tears streaming down his cheeks.

"Sir," he said, "I would like to introduce you to my father."

A Rescue Plan

Friday's father and the pale man, who turned out to be a Spanish seaman, had been captured by the cannibals on the same day. The Spaniard's ship had been wrecked on the mainland during a storm. His Spanish crewmates were now trapped on the coast, unable to return home.

As I turned the roast on the spit to feed our visitors at my hideout, an idea came to my mind. "What if you were to fetch your companions to this island, sir?" I said to the Spaniard. "There is enough timber here to build a new ship. We could sail back home in it."

"An excellent idea," cried the Spanish sailor. "We had two carpenters on board, one of whom survived the storm. I'm sure we could pull it off. We could sail to North America."

Friday's father too was eager to go back to the mainland. His people would also help us build the ship. The cannibals had left one of the canoes behind and the Spaniard and Friday's father climbed into it. Friday carved them new paddles, and we made sure they had enough food and water to last them the journey.

"God speed," I called out after them as Friday pushed the canoe into the water.

"Yes, come back as quickly as you can, Father," said Friday. "We shall look out for you from the hideout."

A Ship at Last

A week passed without news from Friday's father and the Spaniard. But on the eighth day Friday burst into the hideout in great excitement.

"Sir, they are here. They are here."

We ran to the top of the hill. What I spied through my telescope, however, was not the canoe that Friday's father and the Spaniard left in. And nor could it be the Spaniard's crewmates. It was a merchant ship with three masts, and it was flying an English flag. I nearly fainted with joy. After twenty-seven years, I was to be with people from my own country again.

A small boat had been lowered into the water from the ship and was rowing towards the shore. I counted eleven men on the boat. And then I noticed something peculiar. Three of them had their hands tied behind their backs, and the others were watching them closely.

We crept down to the creek and watched as the boat came ashore. The prisoners were tied up under a tree, their captors laughing and treating them roughly.

"Do you think there is fresh water nearby?" I heard one of the captors say. "My throat is parched."

"Let's go and find out," came the reply.

The men made sure their prisoners were tied securely and set off towards the jungle. Here was my chance to save the unlucky ones. I waited until the sailors had disappeared, then stood up and raced down to the beach.

"Good morning, gentlemen," I said to the prisoners. Their jaws dropped open when they saw me, dressed as I was in furs, and followed by Friday.

"You seem to be in some distress," I added. "Can my man and I be of any help?"

The men, still too amazed to speak, nodded. I took out my knife and quickly freed them. They leaped to their feet, all of them rubbing their wrists where the rope had chafed the skin.

"And who do I have the pleasure to be speaking to?" asked one of them, who I noticed was dressed in finer clothes than the other two.

"My name is Robinson Crusoe," I replied. "I am an Englishman. I was stranded here twenty-seven years ago."

"I am the captain of the ship you see there," said the man. "These here are my first mate and a fare-paying passenger. Those rascals who brought us here were part of my crew, but they mutinied and took over my ship. They brought the three of us here to be left to die."

"And is there anyone on board who might still be on your side?" I asked the captain.

"Yes, there are perhaps three or four who were too scared to fight for me, but they would do so if they thought I had a chance of winning," replied the captain. "Two of them are with those here on the island now."

"Then let us try and recapture your ship," I said.

Ambush

Friday told us that the rebels were up near the stream, feasting on fruit.

I gave weapons to the captain and the other two. Friday led us to the spot where he'd seen the villains. They were still eating, and we had no problem in surprising them.

In the ambush, two of them were killed. We managed to tie up the others and take them to a cave. Then we heard the boom of a cannon coming from the merchant ship. I peered through the telescope and saw that the men on the ship had raised a red flag.

"They are wondering why their friends have not returned," said the captain.

Then a second boat rowed for the beach, and I counted ten men in it. The captain borrowed the telescope.

"One of them is Will Atkins, the leader of the mutiny," he said. "Three of the others are still loyal to me. As for the rest, I fear they are criminals too. We stand no chance of regaining my ship. I reckon there are twenty-six more men left on board."

"There are five of us here, and two more we can rely on in the cave," I said. "That makes seven, plus the three you say are loyal to you in the boat approaching now. That makes ten of us. It will be dark soon. These men are on foreign ground, but Friday and I know the island like the back of our hands. Listen, I have a plan."

Recapturing the Ship

As the second boat reached the island and the men got out, our little party retreated back into the jungle. We shouted at the top of our voices, pretending to be the first boatload of rebels to confuse our enemies.

"We are here." "No here." "How do we cross this stream?" "I am trapped! Help! Help!"

The trick worked and they went off in different directions. Before long, my men and I found two of the villains. One I felled with my sword. The other pleaded, "Spare me, I beg you." Then Friday and the captain captured and tied up three more.

By now it was pitch dark. The villains were confused and called out to each other.

"Make it back to the boat if you can," called out a voice.

"That must be Will Atkins," whispered the first mate. "He is dangerous. We must be careful."

The five remaining mutineers eventually made it back to the boat on the beach.

In darkness we crept across the sand and, once close to the villains, jumped up with a wild shout. They were so startled, most of them dropped their guns. Will Atkins fell to his knees begging for mercy.

Some of the men, spotting their captain, came forward. "We are with you, sir," they said.

Will Atkins and the rest of the rebels were tied up and dragged to the cave to join our other prisoners.

"Now, for the second part of my plan," I said to the captain. "You and the ones still loyal to you must return to the ship. You will surprise the villains on the ship and overpower them." And I explained exactly what they should do…

The boats were pushed out and the men rowed to the ship. By now the moon had come out and I could see their progress clearly.

The captain's boat approached the ship. One of the sailors pretended to be a mutineer and called out to the two men guarding the ship. "Ahoy there, we have rescued the others from the island."

A rope ladder was lowered, and the captain leaped on deck. He floored the first man, the ship's carpenter, with the butt of his musket. The second was grabbed by the first mate and gagged before he could cry out.

More men clambered up from the boats and locked the hatches on the deck to trap the sailors below.

The captain advanced to the main cabin where the leader of the mutineers still on board was asleep, guarded by two of his brutes and a cabin boy. The first mate broke down the door with an axe. Caught by surprise, no one in the main cabin was able to put up a fight.

Some time later, I heard the roar of six cannons. It was a signal from the captain. The ship was saved. I waited on the shore until I saw a boat rowing back. The captain had brought me gifts of cake and wine – delights I had not tasted for nearly twenty-eight years.

Rescued at Last

We feasted well into the early hours of the morning, my new friends dancing and playing music on the beach.

As the sun came up, I beckoned to Friday. My time to leave the island had come at last, and I wanted to know what his plans were. Friday decided he wanted to come with me. We would travel to England, and then set off to Brazil where my plantation was.

As we sailed away from my little island, I turned to look at it for the last time. The mutineers were huddled on the shore, glaring at us on the deck. The captain had wanted to hang them, but I'd convinced him to leave them marooned on the island instead. I left them my tools and tent, as well as my herd of goats and pets. The only thing I did not tell them about was the secret cave filled with ammunition. I knew they'd find it soon enough. Friday came to stand beside me.

"Have you said goodbye to our home?" I asked.

"Yes, sir," he replied. "We have had some incredible adventures on our little island. Who knows what other adventures we will have in the big wide world!"

46

About the author

Daniel Defoe is thought to have been born in London
in 1660. The son of a butcher, he witnessed the Black Death
of 1665 and the Great Fire of London in 1666 when he was
a child. He served in the army and was also the king's secret
agent. He wrote pamphlets on all sorts of subjects, and was
even punished in public and put in prison for some of the
things he wrote. He also started two newspapers and wrote
many books, including some of the very first novels
in English. He died in 1731 at about the age of 71.
Robinson Crusoe was based on the real experience of a
sailor called Alexander Selkirk who was marooned on
an uninhabited island for five years from 1704.

Other titles in the Classic Collection series:

Alice's Adventures in Wonderland • *Little Women*
The Three Musketeers • *Treasure Island* • *Pinocchio*
20,000 Leagues Under the Sea • *Heidi* • *The Wizard of Oz*
Gulliver's Travels • *Robin Hood* • *Tom Sawyer* • *Black Beauty*
The Secret Garden • *Anne of Green Gables* • *The Little Princess*

QED Project Editor: Alexandra Koken
Editor: Maurice Lyon • Designer: Rachel Clark
Copyright © QED Publishing 2013

First published in the UK in 2013 by
QED Publishing, A Quarto Group company,
230 City Road, London EC1V 2TT
www.qed-publishing.co.uk

A catalogue record for this book is available from the British Library.

ISBN 978 1 78171 113 2

Printed in China